E PETTY
Petty, Dev,
Claymates /

CLAYA

Written by
DEV PETTY

Illustrated by
LAUREN ELDRIDGE

Ⓛ Ⓑ Little, Brown and Company
New York   Boston

TA-DA!

Peanuts!

You're a heavy peanut.

WHOOPS!

Got your trunk!

You don't need a trunk when you're a...

Pig-e-phant!

Too big.

Boom!

Hurry! You have to
fix yourself, too.

There.
Perfect.

What are you supposed to be again?
An owl.
Really?
Yes!
I don't want to shock you, but—

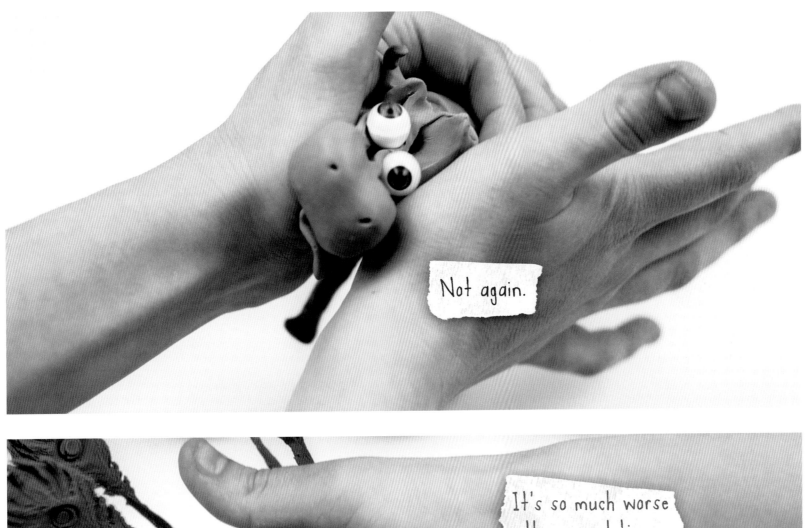

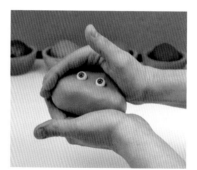

Something wonderful.

ARTIST'S NOTE

I keep a sheet of paper at my desk that reads *Emotion, Movement, Connection.* This reminder helps me look beyond fussy det▮ when I'm making something new. I find that it's not so much how realistic or awesome a character looks but rather how—as a part▮ a scene—that character tells an engaging story. And that means focusing on these three important words.

I used polymer clay, acrylic doll eyes, tinfoil, and wire to create the many shapes of the gray and brown claymates. For the pro▮ set pieces, and so on, I used objects from around my house, such as a bulletin board and a desk lamp, to design the "stage" of ▮ story. When ready to photograph an image, I'm concerned with how something looks only from a very specific angle, so I can ▮ use things like squirt guns, clothes hangers, and cardboard to help me create a desired effect—and I'm the only one who knows t▮ they're there.

Art and stories can be made out of anything! What will you create today?

—Lauren Eldri▮

ABOUT THIS BOOK

This book was edited by Deirdre Jones and designed by Nicole Brown, with art direction by David Caplan. The production ▮ supervised by Erika Schwartz, and the production editor was Jen Graham. The text was set in Agent 'C.'

logo are trademarks of Hachette Book Group, Inc. • The publi▮ is not responsible for websites (or their content) that are ▮ owned by the publisher. • First Edition: June 2017 • Lib▮ of Congress Cataloging-in-Publication Data • Na▮ Petty, Dev, author. | Eldridge, Lauren, illustrator. • ▮ Claymates / written by Dev Petty; illustrated by La▮ Eldridge • Description: First edition. | New Yo▮ Little, Brown and Company, 2017. | Summary: "▮ balls of clay have a great time shaping themse▮ into various animals and objects until their scul▮ comes back and discovers the mess they've m▮ of her work." —Provided by publisher. • Identif▮ LCCN 2015043456| ISBN 9780316303▮ (hardcover) | ISBN 9780316303101 (ebool▮ ISBN 9780316303095 (library edition eboo▮ Subjects: | CYAC: Clay modeling—Fiction▮ Imagination—Fiction. • Classification: LCC ▮ P448138 CI 2017 | DDC [E]—dc23 | LC re▮ available at http://lccn.loc.gov/201504345▮ 10 9 8 7 6 5 4 3 2 1 • 1010 • PRINTED IN CH▮